Welcome to...

THE MAMMOTH ACADEMY

ACADEMY

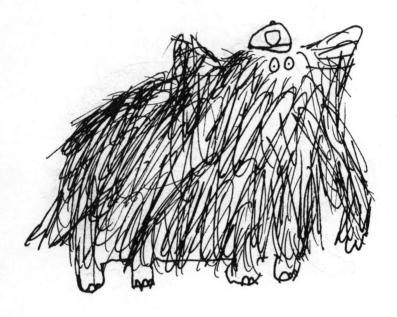

OSCAR WAS

A WOOLLY MAMMOTH.

AND SO WAS

ARABELLA.

SOME OF THE OTHER PUPILS AT THE MAMMOTH ACADEMY

← FLY LIVED IN THE ACADEMY BUT WASN'T A ~~PUPIL~~ PUPIL.

CAVE CAT

ORMSBY

OWL

PRUNELLA

FOX

A FEW MORE PUPILS OF
THE
MAMMOTH
ACADEMY

RHONDA

REGINALD

ROGER

REMI

REX

RUFUS

REENIE

GIANT
GROUND
SLOTH

CAVE
BEAR

Some of the PUPILS OF The ...

PROFESSOR UGH

Professor UGH teaches THE PUPILS of the CAVE SKOOL

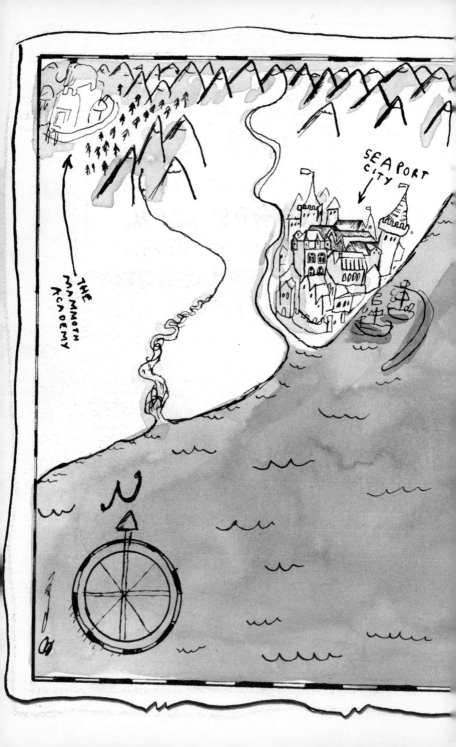

THIS WAY
TO THE
MAMMOTH
LANDS

For Max, Oscar and the Dutch Doctor

Other books in the Mammoth Academy series:

978 0 340 93029 8

978 0 340 93030 4

978 0 340 93031 1

CHAPTER 1
THE NEW STUDENTS

Oscar was a woolly mammoth. He was a student at the Mammoth Academy.

As usual he and all his friends had received a very important letter by Mammoth Mail.

HERE IT IS ↓

Dear Student,

The new term is about to begin very soon and it is one of the most difficult in the year.

All pupils should bring with them:

More exercise books than usual, about twice as many, as you will be doing much more writing this term.
Three large bottles of ink.
A mammoth calculator to help with all the very complicated sums you will be doing this term.
A mammoth slide rule to help with all the very complicated sums you will be doing this term.
A telescope for Astronomy class.
And your prepared 'What I did in the Holidays' talk, ready to present to the rest of the class on the first day back.

The headmistress's Welcome Back meeting will begin at 9.00am in the Great Hall.

Signed,

On the first day back Oscar and Fox were late.
In the distance, beyond the almost-impossible-to-
cross-glacier and the icy wastes, they could see
Arabella and all the other pupils arriving at the
Mammoth Academy gates. But Oscar was in no
hurry to get there. He was moaning to Fox.

'This term is not looking like it will be any fun
at all,' he said. 'There are no study trips and all the
humans have moved miles away now so there's no
chance of an adventure. It's just going to be boring
lesson after boring lesson.'

'But it's good the humans have moved away,' said Fox. 'They were scary, and besides, what about tuba lessons? They sound like good fun.'

club

'I didn't take that option; I've ended up doing double Difficult Sums with Dr K instead.'

'Oh,' said Fox.

Club

Just then they noticed two small figures even further behind, struggling under the weight of an enormous package. Neither Fox nor Oscar recognized them.

Oscar and Fox decided to shuffle a bit slower to let the pair catch them up.

'We're late anyway,' said Oscar. 'What difference is another couple of minutes going to make?'

    As the pair got nearer Oscar and Fox could
see that they were mini woolly mammoths. They
looked about the same age as Oscar, but they were
much, much smaller; instead of being the size of a
normal mammoth, about eight or nine metres, they
were only two or three metres high.

    'Hello, are you going to the Mammoth
Academy?' asked Oscar.

'Would you like a hand with that parcel? It looks very heavy,' said Fox.

'Radical, yes, please,' they replied.

'My name is Simon and this is my younger sister Simone.'

'We're new students. As you can see, the uniforms don't quite fit us but my mum said she'd adjust them when we get home tonight.'

Simon and Simone asked Oscar and Fox what the Mammoth Academy was like as they had never been to a school that big before.

So for the rest of the journey Oscar, with a little help from Fox, told them all about life at the academy…

Before long they had arrived at the academy but by now they were very late indeed, and after guiding Simon and Simone to Snout's office, Oscar and Fox said goodbye to their new friends.

'Thanks for helping carry this,' said Simon.

'These are our surfboards for our *What We Did in the Holidays* talk,' said Simone.

'Oh really! That's what my tuba is for,' said Fox. 'What are you bringing, Oscar?'

Oscar looked very pale. 'Oh no! I completely forgot about that! I haven't prepared anything!'

CHAPTER 2
THE WELCOME SPEECH

By the time Oscar and Fox arrived at the great hall the headmistress's speech had already begun.

'This term is going to – *ahem* – so nice of you to join us, Oscar and Fox. If you'd like to find a seat as quickly as possible I'll continue, and perhaps afterwards you can explain to me why you were late,' she said.

'As I was saying… This term is going to be very difficult. There is a lot to learn, so I want maximum effort from all of you.

'We also have to welcome two new students to the academy: Simon and Simone. They will be studying with us whilst their parents do some important work in the area.

'Simon and Simone are from a different part of the Mammoth Lands, a small island far far to the east.

'They are pygmy mammoths, which, as I'm sure you will all notice, is why they are so much smaller than most of you. Where they come from all mammoths are that size. Now, I want all of you to welcome them warmly and help them feel at home.'

There was lots of whispering in the hall and then Simon and Simone entered from a side door with Professor Snout.

CHAPTER 3
SURF DUDES

Simon and Simone were glad that they had met Oscar and Fox. To them the academy was a bewildering place where everybody else seemed to know where to go and what to do.

'Don't worry, you'll soon get the hang of it,' said Arabella. 'I'm sure you'll have a good stay here. Just let me know if either of you want me to style your wool,' said Prunella.

Meanwhile the news of the pygmy
mammoths' arrival had spread throughout the
academy.

'Don't worry,' said Simon. 'All this whispering
about us has happened alot since we moved to this
part of the mountains.'

And then BONG! BONG! BONG! BONG! It was time for their first lesson with Professor Snout.

'Hello, everybody. Today, before we start the busy term, we're all going to present our *What I Did in the Holidays* talk to the rest of the class. Who would like to go first?

'Ahh yes, Arabella seems keen.'

Arabella's talk was all about skiing. Simon and Simone were fascinated. They had never seen skiing before.

'Radical! We don't have snow or skiing where we come from.'

Some of the other mammoths sniggered.

Next Fox gave his talk all about his new tuba.

'This is a tuba and I practised all summer on it and now I can get a note out of it. PAAAAARRRRRRP! And this term I'm looking forward to tuba lessons where hopefully I'll learn to get some more notes out of it. PAAAARRRRRRRP!'

Simon and Simone were fascinated. They had never seen tubas before.

'Awesome! We don't have tubas where we come from.'

There was some sniggering from the rabbits at the back.

AWESOME!!

'Who's next?' said Professor Snout. 'How about you, Oscar…'

'Erm um…'

Oscar began to look very uncomfortable.

The rabbits began to snigger a lot more until a small voice piped up.

'Erm, I'm afraid Oscar won't be able to give his talk this morning as he agreed to help us carry the things we needed for our talk and help us with our talk, which meant he couldn't carry the things he needed for his talk.'

'I see. In that case perhaps you would like to help Simon and Simone give their talk today, and we can hear all about what you did in the holidays tomorrow,' Professor Snout replied.

Simone began. 'This is the island where we come from.'

'In the holidays we went fishing,' said Simon.
'And we also went canoeing,' said Simone.

'But most of all we went surfing,' exclaimed
Simon. 'Here are our surfboards.'

'This is a handstand.'

'And this is a switch spinner.'

'And here is a trophy we won… and a photo of us surfing.'

'And this is called wiping out… surfing can be very dangerous…! Agggh!'

All the class applauded; none of them had ever seen surfing before.

'Radical!' said Oscar.

CHAPTER 4
LESSONS AND LETTERS

On the way to their next lesson Oscar caught up
with Simon and Simone.

'Thanks loads for helping me back there.
Tiki-Tiki looks amazing and surfing looks really
cool!'

'Don't mention it. It's the Tiki-Tiki way to be
friendly and helpful to other people. And if you ever
come to stay on our island we can teach you how to
surf. It's easy once you know how.'

'Wow, thanks. That would be awesome,' Oscar
replied.

Unfortunately the rest of Oscar's lessons that morning weren't quite as much fun.

First he had double Difficult Sums with Dr K.

'Everyone with me so far…?

'Oh, before you go here is your homework.'

'Don't worry,' said Arabella. 'I'm sure we'll all get the hang of this eventually.'

Next was Astronomy with Dr Van Der Graph.
'This should be more fun,' said Oscar.
'We won't be able to see any stars with
telescopes this afternoon because it's not night-time,
so you can read these books about stars instead.'

49

And then it was time for Human Studies with Professor Biscuits.

Simon and Simone had never heard of humans before.

'There are none on the island where we come from,' said Simon.

'Now, as I'm sure you'll all remember, humans look like this.'

'They are wild and dangerous creatures. They smell because they don't wash much. Their young cubs go to something they call "Cave Skool" where they learn to grunt and bash things. And they eat mammoths, mice, rabbits, giant sloths and pretty much ANYTHING they can get their hands on.'

Simon and Simone began to look a little scared.

'But thankfully,' said Professor Biscuits, 'all the humans seem to have migrated away from the academy lands. So there aren't any humans around here any more.'

Simon and Simone began to look relieved.

'Which is also why this will be your last Human Studies lesson,' said Professor Biscuits. 'With the humans having moved away from here the academy feels it isn't worth teaching you about them. So from tomorrow you'll all have extra double Difficult Sums with Dr K instead.'

Oscar groaned. 'I don't believe it,' he said.
'This is turning out to be the worst term ever...'

There were plenty of other things for Simon and Simone to learn.

Prunella showed Simone the most stylish way to brush her wool.

And Fox showed Simon how to make a snowball.

Some afternoons Simon and Simone would
tell them of their home, and what it was like living
there.

AWESOME!

WOW!

Oscar was fascinated. He loved hearing about the waves, the fishing, the salt and the spray but most of all the *surfing*.

He tried to imagine what it must feel like, kind of like sledging, but on water. In fact he spent most of the rest of the day thinking about it…

'Oscar. OSCAR!' said Professor Snout. 'Did you hear what I just said? I was asking you if you had brought in your prepared *What I did in the Holidays* talk? You're the only member of the class that hasn't presented it yet.'

'Erm. Well, I haven't quite got everything collected for it yet... Perhaps I can do it tomorrow?'

That break-time Fox asked Oscar what he was
going to do for his talk.

'Well, I'm not sure yet. I'll sort it out later.
Look, there's Simon and Simone. Let's go and chat
to them instead…'

Over the next few days Oscar had several different excuses for Professor Snout explaining why he hadn't brought in his *What I did in the Holidays* talk yet.

First of all a woolly warthog ate his paper. Then it snowed.

A sabre-toothed seal took his pencil thinking it was a fish, and swam away with it.

And a herd of wild buffalo knocked over his desk, spilling ink all over it.

It was also taking him a while to find all the *very special things* he needed to present the talk as it was going to be *very* involved.

Until finally, whilst noticing the look on Professor Snout's face, he agreed to bring it to the next lesson without fail.

The next morning on the way to school Oscar was
deep in thought. He was wondering what to do.
He hadn't finished preparing his talk yet, or even
properly started it. It wasn't that he didn't want to
do it, it was more that he didn't know where to start,
and the holidays were so long ago that he couldn't
even really remember exactly *what he had done*.

Just then he noticed that Simon and Simone were walking alongside him looking very glum. They were looking at something.

'Hey, what have you got there?' he asked Simon.

'It's the *Tiki-Tiki Times*,' they replied. 'A new species of animal has been discovered there.'

'Wow, that sounds really exciting! Why are you looking so glum about it?'

'Our parents have had to go back there to help organize things for it,' said Simon.

'They'll be there for a few days, and in the meantime there's nobody to look after us, so we'll have to stay overnight in the academy on our own,' added Simone.

'Oh,' said Oscar.

The Tiki-Tiki Times

NEW SPECIES DISCOVERED!

Fishermen may have sighted a new species of animal off the coast of Tiki-Tiki. The animals seem to be very shy so there are no photographs yet. The king has said that the animals will be given a full Tiki-Tiki welcome should they decide to alight on the island. This may be the most important discovery of recent times say scientists blah blah blah etc blah blah blah blah blah etc etc blah blah blah blah blah etc blah blah blah blah blah etc etc blah blah. blah blah

Then Oscar had an idea.

'Why don't I ask Professor Snout if I can stay
overnight too? I know the academy like the back
of my trunk and it would be fun, like camping, but
indoors, and it would certainly brighten this term up
a bit.'

CHAPTER 5
NIGHT-TIME IN THE ACADEMY

Professor Snout said it was a bit irregular but after some persuasion he agreed to let Oscar stay with Simon and Simone in the academy on the condition that he 'look after them and definitely not forget to present his talk to the class tomorrow.'

At the end of the school day there was one last warning from Professor Snout, 'I want you all to be on your BEST behaviour. And should you have any problems, call the caretaker. He'll be there all the time.'

And so they found themselves alone in the academy.

With no pupils around, the Mammoth Academy was very quiet indeed and, although there was no need, Oscar, Simon and Simone found themselves whispering.

A bit later on they noticed the caretaker's light go out.

'Shhh! We'll have to be really quiet now…'

'What are you going to do for your talk tomorrow?' asked Simon.

'I'm not sure yet. I'll sort it out later. There's plenty of time,' Oscar replied. Anyhow that's boring. Why don't we have another look at the *Tiki-Tiki Times* instead.'

'Good idea!'

Oscar shone his torch so they could read it.

'Look, this is the town where we live,' said Simon

'Wow, radical,' said Oscar.

'Look, here's some more about the new animal.'

Oscar saw it and was shocked.

BIG SWELL EXPECTED

SURFERS ARE LOOKING FORWARD
TO THE BIGGEST WAVE EVER !!!

'That looks like a human footprint!'

'But that's impossible,' said Simon.

'There aren't any humans on our island,' said Simone.

'There never have been.'

'Well, it looks exactly like a human footprint,' said Oscar.

They went on to read more of the article.

'Canoe! That looks exactly like a human in a canoe! The humans must have learnt how to make primitive canoes, and paddled there from the mainland.'

'Wait there's more on the next page…'

A PHOTO OF THE STRANGE NEW ANIMAL SIGHTED IN COASTAL AREAS

THE KING + QUEEN OF TIKI-TIKI ARE
TO HOLD A SPECIAL PARTY TO WELCOME
THE SHY CREATURES TO THE ISLAND.
ALL ISLANDS ARE WELCOME TO
ATTEND.
"WE WANT TO GIVE THESE ANIMALS
A PROPER TIKI-TIKI WELCOME!"
SAYS KING.

'No way! THIS IS TERRIBLE! They can't
welcome the humans like that! They'll be the ones
ending up on the menu. The humans will eat them
all up, every last one.'

Simon and Simone looked very pale and worried. 'This newspaper is dated yesterday, so that means the party is tomorrow. They have to be warned…'

'We must leave tonight,' they both said.

For a moment Oscar looked dumbstruck. What?!!! Leave the safety and warmth of the academy in the middle of the night, travel many mammoth miles to an island he had never been to before to battle with humans…

Then he thought about his lesson tomorrow with Professor Snout, and the talk he *hadn't* prepared...

And besides, his new friends needed his help.
He couldn't let them down.

'OK,' he said. 'I'm in. But how are we going
to get there?'

'I've an idea,' said Simon. 'If you go to Cook's
kitchen and collect some food and water and three
large tablecloths, Simone and I will sort out the
transport. But be quiet. We don't want to wake the
caretaker. If he wakes up he won't let us go.'

Ten minutes later after leaving a hastily written note, the three of them stood outside shivering in the moonlight and Oscar began to wonder if this was such a good idea after all.

'Once we get to the river things should be easier,' said Simon.

CHAPTER 6
NIGHT JOURNEY

It wasn't easy carrying such huge objects to the river. First they had to cross the icy wastes. Then they had to cross the almost-impossible-to-cross-glacier.

As they walked higher up in the forest they could hear wolves howling.

Going downhill was easier than going up, but
eventually they got to the river.
   Simon and Simone launched their surfboards.

'Right, this is your board, Oscar. On you get.'

Oscar had never been on a boat before, let alone a surfboard…

'Don't wriggle!' said Simone.

'Where did you get it from?' asked Oscar. 'I thought you only had two boards.'

'It's Snout's desk,' said Simon. 'I had to modify it a bit, but it will be ideal.'

And he handed Simone and Oscar the tablecloths.

'We can use these as sails.'

'This river leads to Seaport City where we can get a boat to Tiki-Tiki, with the flow of the river and sail power we should get there in no time at all...' said Simone.

'We are going to be in so much trouble...' muttered Oscar.

And so they travelled onwards through the night.

CHAPTER 7
ALL AT SEA

Huddling under blankets they were glad when eventually the sun rose and it started to get a little warmer.

The river had also started to pick up pace, so with the sails billowing in the wind, they began to make good progress.

'Look, I think I can see Seaport City!'

'Great! We should easily be able to get a boat to take us to Tiki-Tiki from there,' said Simon.

'And perhaps some muffins,' said Oscar. 'I'm hungry, and we've eaten nearly all the food we borrowed from the kitchen.'

Gradually the river began to pick up
more pace.

'Hey! The river seems to be taking us away
from Seaport City!' exclaimed Oscar.

Simon pointed. 'Oh dear,' he said. 'I think we
might be in spot of bother.'

'What next?' whispered Oscar.

'Well, by my calculations I make Tiki-Tiki that way…' said Simon.

And so they travelled onwards.

First the food ran out. And then the water.
Giant woolly gulls began to circle overhead.
Oscar had never seen giant woolly gulls before.
Nor sharkosauruses.

The three carried on travelling, staring fixedly at the horizon, until eventually Oscar thought he could see a tiny dot of something many miles ahead. 'Land ho!' shouted Simon and Simone.

CHAPTER 8
PIRATES!

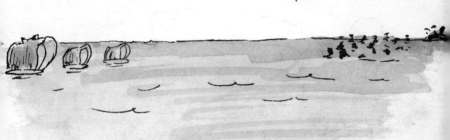

Gradually the little dot on the horizon began to get bigger. The wind had also started to blow a little stronger so they began to make even better progress.

'Yes, that's definitely Tiki-Tiki,' exclaimed Simon. 'Hurray!'

'But what's that in front of it?' asked Simone.

'Let me have a look,' said Oscar. 'I brought my telescope from Astronomy. I thought it might come in useful.

'OH NO! It's HUMANS! IN CANOES!'

'How many of them?' asked Simone in a quavering voice.

'LOTS! And they're HEADING STRAIGHT
TOWARDS THE ISLAND!'

'We'll have to speed up,' said Simon. 'We have
to get there first to warn the islanders.'

'Bigger sails. That's what we need.'

And so they took Cook's tablecloths, their
blankets, and any spare clothes they had and tied
them all together.

'This should do it!' said Simone.

With the bigger sails and the wind blowing more strongly they began to pick up speed. Ahead of them they could see the island and the flotilla of pirates more clearly. There could be no doubt of the humans' intentions.

Or the islanders.
'This is terrible,' whispered Simone.

The wind was blowing even more strongly now.

'It looks like we might make it!' shouted Oscar, when suddenly a massive gust of wind ripped the makeshift sail from his trunk high into the air and out to sea.

'Oh no!' cried Oscar, as his board, in a matter of seconds, began to slow to a standstill…

'Don't worry, Oscar, we'll get you help,' bellowed Simon.

'As soon as we've dealt with the pirates,' added Simone.

And before long Simon and Simone were little dots on the horizon and Oscar found himself alone bobbing in the water.

CHAPTER 9
SURF'S UP!

Oscar began to feel very helpless. He had come all this way to help his friends, and now when they faced their biggest danger he was no use at all.

Using his telescope he could see that Simon and Simone had reached the flotilla. They were skilfully steering their way through the canoes, whilst the humans threw rocks and waved clubs at them.

He could see Simone valiantly throwing anything she could back at them.

But after their initial surprise the humans began to form a circle around Simon and Simone with canoes blocking their way. Several more canoes paddled alongside and humans started leaping on to Simon and Simone's surfboards.

He could see Simon and Simone being tied up.

Oscar looked on, horrified. His friends had been captured and now they would almost certainly be eaten as a snack before the humans went on to eat the rest of the islanders.

And Oscar began to think of his other friends,
the ones he had left behind at the academy: Fox,
Prunella and Arabella…

What would they do in this situation?

Well they wouldn't give up, no matter how difficult or impossible it looked! They'd keep going against all the odds! It was up to him to save Simon, Simone and the islanders. They were depending on him; he had to succeed!

And so Oscar lay down on his board and even though he was so tired he could hardly lift his trunk, he began to paddle.

He was still a very long way from shore. It looked hopeless but he couldn't think of anything else to do.

The flotilla of humans was nearing the shore. It looked like they would definitely get there before him.

And then looking through his telescope Oscar noticed a sudden change come about the islanders. They seemed to have stopped doing their welcome dance and started waving their hands about and pointing.

Perhaps they had seen that the humans had captured Simon and Simone; perhaps they had seen Oscar. Or perhaps the humans were about to eat Simon and Simone! They certainly seemed to be very agitated about something. He had to get there soon or it would be too late…

He carried on paddling even faster than before when he started to notice a low rumbling noise coming from behind him. It was getting louder and louder.

On the shore the islanders were pointing and waving more frantically than before, seemingly in his direction.

The low rumbling noise had turned into more
of a wooshing swoooooshing noise. Oscar looked
over his shoulder to see an ENORMOUS wave
coming towards him.

He started paddling even faster.

'Agghh!'

But the wave carried on getting closer and CLOSER and bigger and BIGGER... sucking up all the water in front of it.

The noise became more and more deafening. With all the salt and spray in his eyes he could hardly see anything...

He could feel himself and the board being lifted high up into the air, until he was right at the top of the wave.

And then all of a sudden the board lurched
forwards and he started to career down the face of it.
'Ahhhhhhheeeeeeeeeeeeeeeee!'
Faster and faster and faster he went.

He decided it might be better to stand up and gradually a big smile came across his face.

'Wheeeeee!'

This was actually fun! By leaning the board left and right he discovered he could make the board turn.

He was SURFING!

'Wheeeeeeeeeeeee! Radical!'

But he had been concentrating so much on
steering he had forgotten to look where he was going.
Suddenly in front of him he saw the first human
pirate boat – he had caught up with them already.
And with a KERRRUNCH! he surfed straight
through the middle of it.

'Ugghh!'

The human pirates were thrown into a state of confusion…

KERRRUNCH! Oscar surfed through another canoe, and then another, and another.

Kerrrunch! KERRUNCH!

The humans started to throw rocks at him… and wave their clubs!

KERRRUNCH!

Then through the salty spray up ahead he could just make out the boat with Simon and Simone on it. They had been tied to the mast and were screaming and shouting.

'Help!'

Oscar started steering towards them. He only had one chance to get this right…

…and KERRRUNCH! He surfed straight through the middle of the boat, reached out his trunk and… caught Simon and Simone!

'Thanks! That was totally radical!' they squealed.

With all three of them on the board it seemed to go even faster; it also became harder to control…

'Woaaahhh!'

'Waaaaaaaaaaa!'

And with a

SPLASHHHHKERRRUNCHGRIIIIIINNND

Oscar, Simon and Simone careered out of the water and straight up the beach, finally coming to a halt in a heap of wet wool, seaweed, sand and bits of surfboard.

As they tried to disentangle themsleves from the mess, the islanders began to circle them, looking confused and a bit frightened. Some of them waved their fishing harpoons at them.

'What is it?' they said.

'I don't know.'

'Perhaps it's some kind of sea monster?!'

'It's us. Simon…'

'…and Simone.'

'And this is our friend Oscar. He's a woolly mammoth too, a mammoth-sized one.'

'They're all this size on the mainland,' explained Simone helpfully.

Just then King Samuel and Queen Samantha arrived.

'Mamma! Pappa!' shouted Simon and
Simone.

'Simon? Simone? Is that you?' shouted the
King and Queen of Tiki-Tiki island.

Oscar couldn't help but be surprised.

'What, you mean your mum and dad are the
King and Queen of Tiki-Tiki?!'

'Yes, we tend to keep quiet about it, otherwise people treat us differently,' said Simon and Simone.

'King Samuel, what shall we do about the rest of these animals?' asked the islanders.

'They're humans,' said Simon.

'They're very dangerous – they eat mammoths,' added Simone. 'They nearly ate us and all of you.'

Simon showed the king a rather soggy exercise book from his Human Studies class.

'Get the fishing fleet out there and round them up before they cause any more trouble,' boomed the king. 'And then do the same as we do with anything else that we catch in the ocean but don't want to eat, throw them back… but make sure you're a very, very long way out to sea…'

And so the entire fishing fleet of Tiki-Tiki launched into the whirling white water. The expert fisherfolk somehow managed to throw nets and manoeuvre amongst the surf, and in no time their nets were bulging.

The rest of the humans, probably realizing that they were no longer welcome, began to swim in the opposite direction as fast as they could.

CHAPTER 10
WELCOME TO TIKI-TIKI

'Now then,' said King Samuel. 'Rather than waste a good welcome feast I propose we give our Tiki-Tiki welcome party in honour of Simon, Simone and Oscar instead.'

A huge cheer went up from the islanders and immediately the celebrations started.

And once they realized that it was Oscar who surfed the giant wave, sank the human fleet, saved Simon and Simone and the island of Tiki-Tiki, he was given a welcome like no other.

Instead of one flower wreath he was given ten. Instead of two glasses of pineapple punch he was given three.

That evening after the excitement of the party had died down, Simon, Simone and Oscar were invited to stay at the Royal Palace.

Simone and Simone asked Oscar if he wanted to go for an evening surf before bed.

'No, I don't think I will,' said Oscar. 'I think I've had enough surfing today, and besides I need to prepare my *What I did in the Holidays* talk for Professor Snout. I've put it off enough already.'

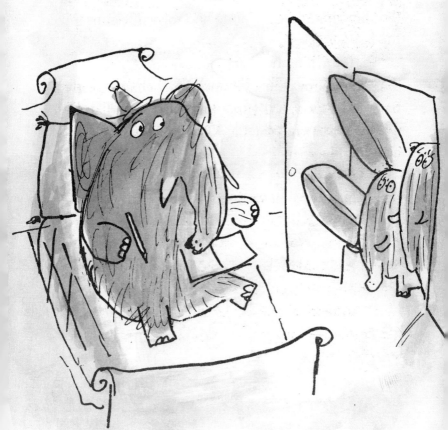

CHAPTER 11
A HERO'S WELCOME

A few days later Oscar, Simon and Simone began the long journey back to the Mammoth Academy. Oscar was hoping to arrive unnoticed. He had an idea that if he sneaked in super casually, and carried on as if nothing had happened, nobody might notice that he, Simon and Simone had missed lessons for the last few days.

Returning by King Samuel and Queen Samantha's royal envoy stopped any chance of that happening though. By the time they arrived at the academy the whole of the Mammoth Lands knew what had happened.

At the gates the headmistress bowed and took a letter from the king's special envoy. She thanked them for safely transporting the students back home and then quietly but firmly asked if Oscar, Simon and Simone might meet her in her office before they started lessons.

Oscar's heart sank.

'We are going to be in SO much trouble!' he whispered. 'Not only did we sneak out of the academy after Snout specifically asked us to be on our best behaviour, but we also turned his desk into a surfboard and lost Cook's tablecloths…'

'I think the best thing we can do is be honest and tell the truth,' said Simon.

'I think you're right.'

There was a moment of silence before the headmistress began.

'Welcome back, you three. I'm glad you arrived safe and sound.

'We found the note you left and I've also
received a letter from Queen Samantha and King
Samuel explaining everything that happened. It
includes an official thank you from the people of the
island of Tiki-Tiki.

'They have also rather kindly sent a brand
new desk for Professor Snout and some beautiful new
tablecloths for Cook.'

'Now, I think you had all better get back to your lessons… You've got a lot of catching up to do. And I believe you have a lesson to attend with Professor Snout, Oscar.'

'That's right,' said Oscar. 'I've got to give my *What I did in the Holidays* talk. Except I haven't prepared a *What I did in the Holidays* talk, so instead it will be more of an *All about the Beautiful Island of Tiki-Tiki and How We Battled the Pirate Humans, Surfed the Biggest Wave Ever and Saved The Islanders From Being Eaten Alive* talk.'

'Do you think Professor Snout will mind?' he said.

'I think it sounds perfect,' said the headmistress.